The Trashy Hootenanny

Sarviol Publishing

ISBN: 978-1500792633

Special wholesale and resale rates are available.
For more information, please contact Deb Harvest
at petethepopcorn@gmail.com

When purchasing this book, please consider purchasing
an additional copy to donate to your local library.

The TRASHY Hootenanny

Written by Nick Rokicki
and Joseph Kelley
Illustrated by Megan "The Cartoonist"

3/2017

Megan & Caleb

Nick Rokicki

Reading is a Hoot!

silly face.

3

Chapter One:

Bethany the Cockroach

"This isn't junk mail! Arrrrghhhh! I only like junk mail!" Bethany the Cockroach huffed as she picked up the envelope that had arrived in the mailbox. Carefully, she read aloud the words, "You are cordially invited to The Trashy Hootenanny…"

Beep! Beep! Beep! Beep! Beep! The smoke alarm was going off, signaling to Bethany that her tofu was properly burned and ready to be eaten. Very quickly, Bethany's three-sectioned body ran to retrieve her meal.

While most cockroaches preferred to consume sweets, meats and even decaying starches, Bethany was a very picky eater. In fact, she was a vegetarian, eating only the

finest rotting fruits, vegetables and other non-meaty foods.

"A hootenanny! I haven't been to a hootenanny in years!" Bethany exclaimed to herself, in between nibbles of her burnt tofu. "There better be lots of moldy, spoiled grapes available… green grapes without skins are the best! Oh! And sour strawberries or stale string beans. The best part about a hootenanny is the food!"

Ppfffffrrrrrrrr. A loud noise escaped from Bethany's backside while a sheepish grin passed across her face. She slowly and deeply breathed in the fresh-smelling gas that was filling the room. That's one of the best things about being a vegetarian, thought Bethany... your house always smells squeaky clean!

With that, Bethany the Cockroach hit the road towards The Trashy Hootenanny.

Chapter Two:

Edward the Slug

What does the clock say? Most would answer, "Tick, tock… tick, tock." But today,

the clock was producing a rather annoying

thumping noise. Thump, thump… thump, thump. "We're gonna be late… thump… I hate being late… thump… time is ticking… thump… where on earth could she be… thump… the hootenanny is gonna start without us… thump… no respect for time… thump," grumbled Edward the Slug, hitting his head on the giant clock near his door. Edward was clearly becoming agitated with his friend, Bethany the Cockroach.

Edward the Slug, as you will come to find out, is a difficult slug to deal with. He lives wherever it is moist, moving homes quite often when the weather becomes dry. This constant moving has made Edward very punctual. However, it has not tamed Edward's tendency to become involved in new things on a regular basis. You could say that he has an addiction to hobbies. In one span of three months, he had taken up coupon-clipping, crafting, growing tomatoes, harvesting honey, painting, canning vegetables, camping and more.

"Yooooooooo-hooooooooooo! I'm here!" came a voice from outside. Bethany the Cockroach had arrived.

"You're late!" shouted Edward, pushing open the door with his slimy body.

"I'm sorry, Edward. You said to be here at 3:00. I think I'm right on time."

"It's 3:02!!!!!!!!!!!!!" howled Edward.

"Calm down, Slugward!"

"Don't call me Slugward, Bethany! We've been over this— my name is Edward and I will not be referred to as Slugwa—."

"Don't get your knickers in a twist," said Bethany, cutting Edward off in mid-sentence. "We have to be on our way to this hootenanny."

With that, Edward the Slug and Bethany the Cockroach hit the road towards The Trashy Hootenanny.

Chapter Three:

Julian the Maggot

"I'm sorry we're late," explained Edward the Slug.

"Hahahahahahahahahahah... ahhahahahahahahahhaha... this is so funny! I'm laughing out loud! I'm literally rolling on the floor laughing! OMG!" cackled Julian the

Maggot, in between giggling hysterically. Julian was, in fact, rolling on the floor. After all, being a fly larvae doesn't allow him to do much else, right?

"What's so funny? The fact that we're **not** even late?" huffed Bethany, shooting a menacing look towards Edward.

"No... hahahahaha... I'm watching this new show, The Real Insects of New York City. It's hilarious! All these bugs just keep feuding and talking about each other. In this episode, the beetle actually flipped over her egg carton!" said Julian.

"Hmmmm… that doesn't sound too funny to me," said Edward.

"Oh, but it is! You just have to watch it. You'll be hooked."

"I'm very, very busy. I don't really have time for that. Speaking of time, we have to get moving," said Edward, sneaking a peek at the clock.

"Edward, Edward, Edward… always looking at the time. We're all traveling to the hootenanny together, so it can't start without us. Just calm down," interjected Bethany.

"Hey, did you see on the news about President Paper Wasp? He might show up at the hootenanny!" said Edward.

"Nah, I don't really watch the news," said Julian. "It's way too boring."

"You really should try to keep up on current events, Julian," said Bethany. "You just never know when something in this world is going to affect you directly. There could be a water shortage or hurricanes or disease or fires or…"

"I get it, Bethany. Let's get going. My show is over," said Julian. "I just hope my DVR records all the episodes while I'm gone."

With that, Julian the Maggot, Edward the Slug and Bethany the Cockroach hit the road towards The Trashy Hootenanny.

Chapter Four:

Genevieve the Louse

"But I don't get it. Is she a lice or a louse? Are they two different things? I've never even heard of a louse. Of course, I've heard of a lice. They're so pretty," said Julian the Maggot as the trio of friends approached the home of Genevieve the Louse.

Bethany rolled her eyes as Edward explained the difference to Julian. "A louse is

the same thing as lice. Lice is plural for louse. The reason that you usually hear 'lice' instead of 'louse' is because they normally travel in packs," said Edward.

"But Genevieve is very shy— so please don't ask her why her friends aren't coming," said Bethany, just before knocking on Genevieve's door.

When the door slowly opened, Julian gasped as he got his first glimpse of Genevieve the Louse. If there ever were such a thing as a pretty louse, Genevieve was it. There she stood, wearing her eyeglasses and carrying a small handbag.

"Hi Gen," said Bethany. "These are my friends, Edward and Julian. They're both very excited to meet you!"

"That's a very nice blouse you're wearing," said Julian. "A pretty blouse for a pretty louse!"

Genevieve lowered her head as she tried to hide her grin. "Thank you! I bought it at InsectMart," she said. "I wanted to get something new for the hootenanny, but I didn't want to be too fancy."

"I think you look simply adorable, Genevieve," complimented Bethany.

"Who do we have to pick up next?" questioned Genevieve.

"Just come on, you'll see," warbled Julian.

"You know I don't like surprises!" exclaimed Edward.

With that, Genevieve the Louse, Julian the Maggot, Edward the Slug and Bethany the Cockroach hit the road towards The Trashy Hootenanny.

Chapter Five:

Francesca the Rat

"I've never been in this neighborhood before. Is it safe?" questioned Genevieve as she straightened her glasses.

"Oh, you'll be fine," whispered Edward.

"Then why in the heck are you whispering?" wondered Genevieve.

"Pay them no mind. We're almost there. Her place is right over this way, by that hole in the fence," explained Julian.

Bethany, Edward, Julian, and Genevieve were all greeted with a mat near the hole in the fence. The letters W-E-L-C-O-M-E were arranged neatly across the filthy mat.

"What does that spell?" asked Bethany.

"You don't know what that says?" laughed Julian.

"Stop laughing at her Julian, that is rude," said Edward. "The letters spell the word *WELCOME*, Bethany."

"Why, oh why, are my feet sinking into this mat?" Bethany hollered.

"Is someone there?" asked an unknown voice, from inside the hole.

"It's us! We're here to pick you up to go to the hootenanny. Please don't make us late," said Edward as he looked at his watch, not-so-neatly duct-taped to his wrist. "Francesca, you know that you're the only rodent that has been invited to the hootenanny. Do not waste this opportunity that you have been granted."

Minutes passed by before whiskers appeared from the dark hole. Soon thereafter, a plump grey body, accompanied by a long, dirty, pinkish tail made its way though the hole. On the tail was some sort of brown paste.

"Is that peanut butter?" asked Julian the Maggot.

"Oooohhhh, I love peanut butter!" said Genevieve.

"All this talk about peanut butter is making me hungry!" bellowed Bethany.

"Sorry everyone, I just had to use the bathroom," explained Francesca the Rat, yawning, stretching and then yawning once more. "Man alive! That made me tired!"

With that, Francesca the Rat, Genevieve the Louse, Julian the Maggot, Edward the Slug and Bethany the Cockroach hit the road towards The Trashy Hootenanny.

Chapter Six:

Annabelle the Giant Water Bug

"Bethany! Please don't fall in the water!!!!" Edward the Slug said, clearly frightened for his friend as she tiptoed near the edge of the pond.

"Oh, Edward... I'm fine! We just have to find out which plant Annabelle is living near right now," said Bethany.

"Which plant? Living near? Right now? What do you mean? She's a drifter? A wanderer?" asked Francesca. "Is she homeless? A vagrant? A transient? A floater? A rolling stone? A stree…"

"We got it! We really, really got it, Francesca!" screamed Edward, interrupting the rat before she could list any more terms describing the lifestyle of Annabelle the Giant Water Bug.

"Annabelle! Annnnnaaaaaaaabellllllllle! Annabelle? ANNABELLE!" roared Bethany,

trying to capture the attention of the water bug near an Amazon Lily, sprouting up through the water.

"Annabelle? Annabelle? Are you over here?" asked Francesca the Rat, leaning out over the water to peek near the Blue Pickerel Weed, growing out of the dark water.

"ANNABELLE! We have to get going!!! Come out, come out, wherever you are!!!" screamed Genevieve the Louse, her tiny louse mouth making the most noise it could. Genevieve chose to look for Annabelle by the Water Hyacinth, an ugly pinkish flower floating above the water.

"Well, I truly do appreciate all of your help with searching for Annabelle, but she is clearly nowhere to be found," said Edward. "I really feel bad about leaving anyone behind, but we've spent quite a bit of time here."

"It is what it is. If Annabelle isn't responsible enough to be here when you asked, then she doesn't deserve a hootenanny… even if it is supposed to be the hootenanny to end all hootenannies," said

Francesca the Rat. "Maybe we can leave her a note with the address? In case she'd like to meet us there?"

"I think that's a splendid idea, Francesca," said Bethany the Cockroach, clapping all of her hands.

"Well, there's one problem with that, ladies," cautioned Edward. "Only Simon the Earthworm knows where the hootenanny is! He's only invited certain people, so he is keeping the location top secret. We won't

know where we're going until we meet Simon
and he takes us there."

"All of us are putting an awful lot of
trust in Simon… what if there isn't a
hootenanny at all?!?!" pondered Genevieve.

"Simon is one of the most honest
creepy-crawlies I know, Genny. I'm sure
everything will work out," said Julian, trying
to calm Genevieve's nerves.

"Time, time, time! Time is money and I
don't waste money. So let's move!" demanded

Edward the Slug. "Perhaps we shall run into Annabelle on the way… but we simply cannot wait any longer!"

With that, Francesca the Rat, Genevieve the Louse, Julian the Maggot, Edward the Slug and Bethany the Cockroach hit the road towards The Trashy Hootenanny.

Chapter Seven:

Krystal the Ant

"I know that Krystal's house is in this next block, in between one of these sidewalk cracks. Her ant hill is one of the biggest on the block!" said Genevieve the Louse, pushing her glasses up her nose in excitement.

"She has a big house? That must mean she's rich!" said Julian.

"Well, I don't know about that, Julian…
but I know it's a whole heck of a lot of sand,"
replied Genevieve.

"If she's rich, she could be on this great
television show called Rich Kids of Ant Hills
— it's one of my favorite programs!"
slobbered Julian, getting himself so hysterical
thinking about his only pastime. "I can't get
enough of it, actually! It's just too, too, too
good! All of these ants have *everything* they
could possibly want! The whole thing is so
obnoxious and entertaining… and
educational, in my opinion."

"Julian, are there any television shows
that you *don't* watch!?!?" asked an
exasperated Edward the Slug.

"Duh! I can't stand *anything* that
concerns news or history or current events or
documentaries or…"

"So basically, *anything* that you can
learn *something* from?!?!" hollered Edward,
interrupting Julian.

"What on earf' be all 'dis racket 'round
here? Y'all be shoutin' n' yellin' and wakin' up

da' 'hood," called a loud, booming voice from inside a nearby mound of dirt. All of the bugs looked at each other, trying to decipher the dialect coming from the mouth of Krystal the Ant. Krystal was emerging from the nearby collection of anthills.

"Whatchu' mean? You sayin' my Mama so ugly she be lookin' like she been done hit wit' da' ugly stick? Well, yo' mama such a troll 'dat she build her house on lava rock!" shouted Krystal, turning back to peek inside of her hill.

Suddenly, a roaring fluttering of wings was heard from above! All of the friends ducked low, towards the ground, peeking up in fear. Sure enough, something was quickly flying directly at them, coming from the street light. Was that — could it be — ?

"Ha! I gotcha! I gotcha!" shouted Annabelle the Giant Water Bug, landing near the assembled group.

"Annabelle — 'dat be triflin'! You 'bout near gimme a heart 'tack!" screamed Krystal the Ant.

"Yes, Annabelle! You shouldn't do that! There are a lot of flying birds that would eat any of us for dinner — you can't go around scaring people," said Edward.

"I just wanted to surprise everyone and I thought it would be funny. I'm sorry," apologized Annabelle.

"Who else we gots' goin' to 'dis Hoo'nan' wit' us?" asked Krystal.

"My name is Francesca... and I'm a rat," said Francesca.

"Humph. You sho' is," said Krystal, shooting Francesca a sideways glance.

"And I'm Bethany!" exclaimed Bethany the Cockroach, trying to be as sweet as could be. Krystal slowly lowered then raised her head, giving Bethany a once-over. Without saying a word, she turned to look at Julian.

"Now, I know you is 'da maggot but 'dis here girl Beffa-knee, her so dirty, it look like 'dey done dug her up straight out 'da dirt!" said Krystal. Bethany huffed and crossed her arms around her chest. She couldn't understand why Krystal would be so mean.

With that, Krystal the Ant, Annabelle the Giant Water Bug, Francesca the Rat,

Genevieve the Louse, Julian the Maggot, Edward the Slug and Bethany the Cockroach hit the road towards The Trashy Hootenanny.

Chapter Eight:

Maddie the Stink Bug

"Everyone, follow me! I know a shortcut to Maddie's house," pronounced Edward the Slug.

"A shortcut? Is it the shortcut that I'm thinking of?" questioned Genevieve the Louse.

"Well… if you're referring to the flowers, yes."

"Oh, Edward, I think we'd all rather just take the long way so we don't have to pass those nasty, bright, stinking, wretched purple flowers," said Genevieve.

"Yeah! And I want to travel the fewest amount of steps. I just hate walking. Walking is exercise and exercise is for walking sticks and I don't see any walking sticks on this trip! I'm only taking the shortcut if someone carries me," complained Francesca the Rat.

"That rat is so lazy… never wants to walk, unless it's to the fridge or the bathroom. And she obviously contradicts herself! If she doesn't want to walk, why wouldn't she take the shortcut?" asked Edward the Slug, to nobody in particular.

"Belch! Excuse me. I think I could carry you, Francesca. If you hold on to my suspenders," stated Annabelle the Giant Water Bug. All of the bugs, plus Francesca the Rat, were talking over each other, holding their own conversations. In the midst of this, laughter erupted from the mouth of Julian the Maggot, as he pointed towards the sky.

"Hahahaha, hahahahaha, hahhahah. Those things are so weird!" laughed Julian.

"What be so funny?" rudely questioned Krystal the Ant. Julian didn't offer any sort of understandable response… because all he could do was continue laughing. "'dat Julian be messed up in 'da head. Weird, he say… 'da only thing weird 'round here is hims!"

"Look! Look!" yelled Bethany the Cockroach and Edward the Slug at the exact same moment. The pair were both gesturing straight ahead, right where Julian the Maggot continued to stare and laugh.

"Yo homeboy, whatchu 'and homegirl pointin' at in 'da sky?" asked Krystal.

"Homegirl? Homeboy? I assume you are referring to Bethany and I?" asked the very-well-spoken and educated Edward, who was becoming visually aggravated.

"Well you two was 'da only ones that be waving yo' hands all 'round and tellin' us all to look," said Krystal.

"Butterflies!" screamed Edward, losing his cool. "We are pointing at butterflies!!!"

"Oh, I be thinkin' butterflies is so ugly! All dose colors! And dose wings! Ugh! 'Dat orange and black one 'dere, wit' 'da white spots, is so ratchet," said Krystal.

"Ratchet? What does 'ratchet' mean exactly?" asked Edward.

"I don' know. She jus' be lookin' like she thinkin' she all special," said Krystal.

"You all go ahead toward the meadow, I have to pee," said Francesca the Rat,

interrupting the back-and-forth between
Krystal and Edward.

"Francesca is right. Let's get moving.
Time is ticking," replied Edward the Slug,
shooting a terse look at Krystal. If it was one
thing that Edward couldn't stand, it was
insects that couldn't form complete sentences.

Slowly, the entire group marched
onward, forming a single file line through a
field of tall grass. Francesca the Rat trailed
behind, sniffing the ground for scraps of food
the others may have dropped. Leading the

pack, like a soldier on a mission, was… you guessed it… Edward the know-it-all Slug. Soon, the grass gave way to an area shaded by bushes of green and purple.

"Oh, gross! That smell! I can barely breathe," coughed Bethany the Cockroach, holding her nose.

"That's gotta be the worst smell ever!" croaked Julian the Maggot.

"Uhhhhhh… I think I'm gonna be sick…" cried Genevieve the Louse.

"Pull it together, it's just the lilacs! We will be out of the bushes soon! Just don't breathe in too deep," said Edward, trying to calm the group. The purple lilacs were in full bloom, providing a wonderful scent that most humans would find delightful and relaxing… too bad the bugs thought differently.

"'Dis smell be funky, Eddie. How we know you tellin' us 'da troof?" asked Krystal.

"The truth? The truth about what?" replied Edward.

"'Dat 'dis shortcut be fo' real," said Krystal.

"Because once you start to see the apple trees… in about two minutes… you'll know that I was right! And don't call me Eddie — ever again!" complained Edward, adjusting his glasses. Sure enough, after exactly two minutes of passing underneath the remaining lilac bushes, the group began to see large red spheres hanging from trees.

"See? I told you so!" said Edward, staring at Krystal.

"Bye, Felicia!" replied Krystal. Edward gave her a quizzical look and shook his head, dumbfounded.

"She lives right by that second apple tree," remarked Annabelle. "I remember because she invited me over to try some homemade rotten peach pie. It was sooooooooo delicious, just the right amount of sour! I even took a piece home in the soda bottle top she had."

Hearing the commotion approaching her favorite apple tree, where she lived underneath in an old mayonnaise jar, Maddie the Stink Bug flew out to greet her guests.

Maddie was a fully-grown adult stink bug, so her body was just as wide as it was long!

"Hi e-ghh-very—ghh—body!" said Maddie, in between trying to chew something in her mouth.

"Why you be eatin' when you be knowin' we on 'da way to 'da Hoo'nan'?" questioned Krystal.

"I'm just so, so, so, so, so, so, so hungry, Krystal! Just a few more bites of these overripe crabapples. There is nothing tastier than overripe crabapples — especially with moldy mayonnaise," said Maddie, chunks of apples spewing out of her stuffed mouth. "I simply can't help myself!"

"Oh, I have a similar recipe that I saw on Dirty Diners, Disgusting Drive-ins and Outhouses. Hahahahahaah! I actually saved the episode on my DVR if you'd like to watch it someday," offered Julian the Maggot, still giggling while remembering the episode of one of his favorite television shows.

"We's gots ta' go!" shouted Krystal the Ant, becoming irritated at the conversation.

"This might be the first and only time, but I agree with Krystal. It is time to proceed," said Edward, sweating profusely while looking at his watch.

"Hahahahahahahahaha!" laughed Julian the Maggot, as he caught a glimpse of his own reflection in Maddie's house.

With that, Maddie the Stink Bug, Krystal the Ant, Annabelle the Giant Water Bug, Francesca the Rat, Genevieve the Louse, Julian the Maggot, Edward the Slug and Bethany the Cockroach hit the road towards The Trashy Hootenanny.

Chapter Nine:

Jacob the Centipede

"How in the heck are we going to get across this lake?" wondered Genevieve the Louse.

"I ain't crossin' no dirty water lake," complained Krystal the Ant.

"I'll bet you one whole week's worth of pumpkin seeds that there's some delectable and delightful treats at the bottom of that lake!" remarked Maddie the Stink Bug.

Krystal couldn't believe what her antennas were witnessing! She's still hungry?!?!? I don't know where she puts it, thought Krystal to herself.

"Everyone, gather around. Let's THINK about this. We are all intelligent and can surely figure out a solution to get across this lake," said Bethany the Cockroach.

"Intelligent?" questioned Annabelle. All the other insects stopped to look at Annabelle,

who stood nearby with a perplexed look on her face.

Gazing around at his friends, Julian the Maggot burst out laughing. One by one, heads turned to look at each other. Nobody could figure out why Julian was laughing… because this cheerful maggot clearly didn't know what the word intelligent meant, either.

"Intelligent! You got that right! We are all very, very hairy," said Annabelle, to nobody in particular. The poor water bug thought that intelligent meant hairy. Annabelle, however, was quite pleased with herself for figuring out the meaning of the word all on her own — without even looking at a dictionary. Edward the Slug overheard Annabelle and rolled his eyes. As much as he wanted to, he didn't correct her. It just wasn't worth his time.

All huddled in a circle, Bethany, Edward, Julian, Genevieve, Francesca, Annabelle, Krystal and Maddie were trying to concentrate and figure out how to cross this lake. By human standards, this wasn't a lake at all… but a puddle formed by a recent rainstorm. In fact, any vehicle could easily drive through it.

Nervously, Genevieve questioned, "Why don't we use leaves to get across? Would that work?"

"Yes, yes, yes, yes! I think she is absolutely correct— and it would be so much fun! This would totally be an episode on my reality show!!!" pronounced Julian the Maggot.

"Where we be gettin' all 'dese leaves from?" asked Krystal the Ant.

"Everyone, search your area for leaves and bring them to the water's edge," announced Bethany the Cockroach.

"Hey, Annabelle," whispered Francesca. "I think I hurt my wrist… could you be so kind to find me a big leaf that will support my weight? Oh— and make it a yellow one? Oh, oh— and a leaf that doesn't have any bug bites out of it?"

"Why, of course, I will!" said Annabelle. Annabelle was a bug that was always willing to help others, no matter how tired she was. Ever since she was just a small water bug, she consistently found pleasure in helping those around her. Watching Annabelle embark on her leaf-finding journey, Francesca figured this was a perfect time to take a disco nap. A disco nap, according to humans, was a short nap required before a night of partying... and that's what the hootenanny was surely going to be!

Searching through tall green grass and twigs, Maddie the Stink Bug yelled, "I've got one. I've got one."

Krystal was about 15 paces away and couldn't quite see what Maddie was holding in her grasp, but it wasn't a leaf. "Why you be holding up that bone when we suppose' to be lookin' fo' leaves?" asked Krystal.

"This isn't just any old bone, Krystal. This is a chicken bone — and it still has meat on it!" said Maddie, taking big bites out of the rotten chicken. Krystal shook her head. Maddie was the hungriest bug that Krystal had ever met.

"That sure is a funny-looking bone! Maybe it's the chicken's funny bone!!! Get it? Get it? Funny bone!!!! Hahahahah hahahah hahahahah," laughed Julian. "I really crack myself up sometimes!"

"You sho' be funny Julian… so funny you needs to be goin' to da' funny farm. That's where my Uncle Larry had to go last summer," explained Krystal to Julian.

The bugs heard a rustling sound coming from behind an old flat tire with a rusted rim that was nearby. Slowly, Annabelle made her way from behind the tire, dragging two leaves behind her. One was green, with just a hint of red showing near the edges, a tell-tale sign of the changing seasons. In the other hand, she held a large, sturdy, thick leaf. It was yellow, just as Francesca had requested. "Do you think this will do?" called out Annabelle, looking towards the rat, who was just waking up from her nap.

"As long as there aren't any bug bites… I can't be taking on water when we cross over that lake!" said Francesca. The rat saw

Annabelle dragging the leaf toward her
instead of toward the lake. She was not about
to lift a finger, if she could avoid it. "Just take
it over by the edge of the water, Annabelle!
I'll meet you there — once I fully wake up!"
said the rat, crossing her arms.

"Does everyone have their leaves?"
asked Edward the Slug. "Just across the lake
is Jacob's house."
"Where he stay?" questioned Krystal.

"If you are trying to ask where Jacob resides, he lives just across the lake, in a pile of leaves surrounding a gnome," said Edward.

"I don't do gnomes," explained Krystal, as she raised five fingers and placed them right in front of Edward's face.

"Ugh! It is simply a ceramic figure of a gnome, which humans put in their gardens to scare away those gorgeous black crows," explained Edward the Slug.

"Oh! Crows love corn," piped in Maddie.

"How you know crows be eatin' corn?" asked Krystal.

"One time at Stink Bug Camp... it was a very hot day," Maddie gasped, becoming so excited she could barely keep breathing and speak at the same time. "And there was corn... and... and... and... the corn hit the hot ground... and I heard a popping noise... and boy, oh boy, was it tasty!!!!"

"Popcorn!!! That's what you ate, Maddie— popcorn. Everybody loves popcorn," clarified Genevieve the Louse.

"ENOUGH! We are going to be late for the hootenanny. Grab your leaves and let's get across while the wind is blowing in our direction," shouted Edward the Slug. Little did Edward know, but the "wind" to which he was referring was actually the air coming from the back end of Maddie the Stink Bug.

One by one, the insects carefully placed their leaves onto the still surface of the water. Gently and ever-so-softly, they each stepped on their leaf and slowly floated across the lake, towards Jacob's pad. The tall gnome

statue appeared before them as they drifted
across the water. The red hat looked to be
twenty stories tall! The long, white beard
gave the gnome a very menacing look. "I can
see why those beautiful birds would be scared
of something so hideous!" said Bethany.

"Jacob, we're here!" announced
Annabelle the Giant Water Bug.

"I'm just putting on my last pair of
tennis shoes— shouldn't be more than a
minute!" yelled Jacob from inside the pile of
leaves surrounding the gnome. Moments later,
all dressed and geared up for his long walk,

Jacob emerged from the pile of leaves to greet his friends. His body was so long, accompanied by 100 sets of feet, that it took him several seconds to fully appear!

"Ooooooohhhhhhh... you gots' some nice legs, Jacob. Do you play b-ball?" asked Krystal.

"Basketball? Oh yeah, I love basketball! I am saving up money, so I can buy 100 pairs of the new Nike Air Jordans! All of the cool centipedes are wearing them!"

"A hunned pairs? Dannnnnnnnng. That's a lots of feets!" said Krystal.

With that, Jacob the Centipede, Maddie the Stink Bug, Krystal the Ant, Annabelle the Giant Water Bug, Francesca the Rat, Genevieve the Louse, Julian the Maggot, Edward the Slug and Bethany the Cockroach hit the road towards The Trashy Hootenanny.

Chapter Ten:

Wesley the Japanese Giant Hornet

"I'm telling you, Wesley is BIG!" declared Jacob the Centipede.

"How big is he?" asked Genevieve the Louse. "I'm so small, I get really scared about things that are a lot bigger than me!"

"I mean, he's a Japanese GIANT Hornet! That should tell you just how big he is!" answered Jacob.

"I'm a Giant Water Bug and I don't think I'm really that big," observed Annabelle, adjusting her suspenders accordingly. All of the bugs stopped and looked up at Annabelle, fluttering her wings above the group. It was clear that Annabelle suffered from bug body dysmorphia — she thought she was smaller than she actually was.

"Genny, you'll be fine! I've met Wesley once before and he's very nice. No matter how big he is, you won't be scared when you meet him," advised Bethany the Cockroach.

"I wish I was big!" whined Genevieve. "Just think of all the things I could do…"

"I wish I *were* big," corrected Edward the Slug.

"Oh, you too?" asked Genevieve.

"No— I'm perfectly fine with the way I am. What I am not fine with is your incorrect usage of the English vocabulary! *I wish I were big* is the correct way to say what you're trying to say!" lectured Edward.

"Do you hear it? Do you? Do you?"
rasped Francesca the Rat, excitedly running
in circles. "That noise has got to be Wesley!"

"Noise? Hornets don' be makin' no
noise, do 'dey?" wondered Krystal the Ant.

"Their wings make noise when they fly
really fast!" gurgled Maddie the Stink Bug, as
she slurped down the remainder of the fat,
juicy caterpillar that she had been keeping in
her pocket.

"Gurrrrrlllllll, I don' know where you
put all 'dat food!" squealed Krystal.

Suddenly, the noise to which Francesca
was referring became loud enough for all to

hear. All eyes to the sky, the group of friends gasped at once, spotting Wesley the Japanese Giant Hornet coming in for landing. When he was five feet from the ground, he dipped and twirled, somersaulting in the air!

"Wow!"

"Awesome!"

"Cool!"

Jacob the Centipede was so excited that he couldn't speak at all! In fact, all you could see was a blur of shoes moving in a circle, seemingly going 100 miles per hour!

"Crazy!"

"Gnarly!"

"Insane!"

The chorus of catcalls from the gang of bugs grew louder until Wesley, finished with his rounds of aerial acrobatics, finally landed. Thunderous applause greeted the Giant Hornet as he tipped his hat and bowed at the crowd surrounding him. Wesley was very big,

after all. Standing on the ground, he was much taller than the other insects and was even able to look eye-to-eye with Francesca the Rat! After soaking in all of the attention, Wesley's eyes settled on Genevieve the Louse.

"Who do we have here?" breathed Wesley, turning to walk to the tiny louse.

"Her name is Genevieve—and she is scared of you. So don't come any closer!" snapped Julian the Maggot, stepping in front of Genevieve, guarding the beautiful louse from Wesley. Genny's eyes were as big as the moon... out of fear? Or something else?

"Genevieve, eh? I mean no harm, my beautiful louse. But when I see a stunning being such as you, I must greet her with kindness and respect," wooed Wesley, casting an evil grin at Julian.

"Oh, enough with the love triangle, already!" interrupted Edward the Slug. "We've got to get going — next stop is the Roach Motel!"

"Da' who motel?" shrieked Krystal.

"It's my family's property! Such a lovely place for weary travelers to rest their eyes after a day of adventure... we have to pick up Alexander," explained Bethany the Cockroach. "It might take a little bit of work getting Alexander to leave the motel. He's so comfortable there that he never ventures out. But we sure have to try — I'd hate for anybody to miss this hootenanny!"

With that, Wesley the Japanese Giant Hornet, Jacob the Centipede, Maddie the Stink Bug, Krystal the Ant, Annabelle the Giant Water Bug, Francesca the Rat, Genevieve the Louse, Julian the Maggot, Edward the Slug and Bethany the Cockroach hit the road towards The Trashy Hootenanny.

Chapter Eleven:

Alexander the Bed Bug

"The Roach Motel is so beautiful! Once I retire, I'm going to move there and help operate the business with the rest of my family," began Bethany the Cockroach.

"There's just something so special about the place… sheets that are only washed for every third guest, brown water flowing freely from the faucets, that refreshing scent of mildew that permeates the air. Oh, it's so lovely."

The line of bugs, along with Francesca the Rat, was slowly proceeding up the long, winding, narrow driveway that led to a strip of motel rooms. High overhead, a sign flickered in the night sky, reading, "The Wayside Motel."

"'Dat sign say sometin' bout' Wayside Motel, not Roaches. You sure we be where Alexander stay?" asked Krystal.

"Oh, yes, yes! The Wayside Motel is the official name for the property. But people love it so much that they've given it the nickname The Roach Motel. I can't count how many visitors throughout the years who have come to the front desk and prattled on and on and on about our Roach Motel. They say they've never seen anything like it and they're going to tell all of their friends!"

Alexander the Bed Bug was quite indecisive when it came to his favorite room at The Wayside Motel. Room Number Nine was nice because it had a vibrating massage bed! Visitors would put in a quarter and then the bed would shimmy and shake! What makes this even better for bed bugs? The people don't even notice the nibbling on their skin with all that movement going on! This bed dates back to the 1970s — and the mattress does, too. Which makes it a favorite party place for The Wayside Motel's resident family of cockroaches.

Room Number Nine might be fine…
but Room Number Ten was cool as a Toledo
Mud Hen! Room Number Ten was
sandwiched in-between Room Number Nine
and the Cleaning Supply Closet. Folks would
always ask to stay in the room because they
figured that the cleanest room was the one
closest to the cleaning supplies! Well, they
were wrong. However, they did get a nice,
quiet night's sleep— since the housekeeping
staff only worked one day per week! And for
Alexander the Bed Bug, soundly sleeping
guests meant dinner would be a snap!

"Housekeeping!" chirped Bethany the Cockroach, as she knocked on the door to Room Number Nine.

"Housekeeping? Housekeeping? Yeah, right! Not in this place!" called Alexander as he came to the door. When Alexander opened the door, there was a flurry of activity in the distant corners of Room Number Nine. It was as if the tiny bit of light coming from the flickering Motel sign had scared something away. "It's alright, guys! It's just your cousin Bethany and her friends. Come on out!"

Sure enough, out of the dark crevices in the room, soon appeared dozens upon dozens of cockroaches. They all chirped and hissed at one another, pointing at their cousin. Bethany was a stranger to them, living as far away as she did. But more so, her cousins didn't know what to think of Bethany's vegetarianism. Most cockroaches weren't picky when it came to food. Some of them even snacked on the hair that guests tended to leave in the sheets of the motel beds — or even on little morsels of food that tend to get stuck in toothbrushes!

"Hey, cousins!" blurted Bethany, her excitement unfazed by the whisperings of her relatives.

"Hi, Bethany," said Angela, the prettiest cockroach.

"What's up, cousin?" asked Constantine, the tallest cockroach.

"I've got some leftover bacon from breakfast, Bethany… Sure you don't want some?" inquired Nathaniel, who was seemingly trying to start something about his cousin's eating habits.

"Now, now, Nathaniel. We all know that cousin Bethany is a weirdo. No need to bring it up again," said a voice from the shadows. Soon, out stepped Bethany's Aunt Ellen, dragging her large body, which was clearly too heavy for her legs.

"Well, that's just plain rude, Madam. We're all free to make our own choices in this life. And if Bethany doesn't like to eat meat, then that is her decision. From the look of things, you might want to add some vegetables to your diet!" Turning swiftly to

Alexander, the redness in his face easing, Edward continued, "Now, are you ready to go, young man? The hootenanny starts first thing in the morning… and we still have two stops to make."

"Hmmmmm… I don't know. Maybe I'm not gonna go. I hate to be away from home, ya' know," hesitated Alexander. "I just think I should stay here. We've got some real filthy guests staying here tonight — with kids! That's when we always find the best stuff. Plus, I still have to go fold the toilet paper."

"Fode' 'da TP? Whatchu' be fodein' TP fo'?" pondered Krystal.

"You know when you stay at hotels and motels, and there is a little V-shape in the toilet paper? The bed bugs and cockroaches work as a team to do that," said Alexander. "That's how you know when you're staying in a real classy place."

"While all of this is very interesting, are you coming or not?" asked Edward.

"Will they have blood at the hootenanny?" wondered Alexander.

"Oh, come on, Alexander! Live a little! What good is sitting alone in your room? Come, hear the music play! Put down the knitting, the book and the broom!" pleaded Wesley the Japanese Giant Hornet.

"Ummmm… Wesley, that's from a Broadway musical. Cabaret? You must enjoy Broadway musicals…" oozed Julian, a sly grin on his face.

"There's nothing wrong with that!" blustered Wesley, puffing out his chest, hands on his hips. "Perhaps you could use a little culture, TV boy! I want to write musicals or even a book for children when I grow up. I've

got much bigger plans than sitting around watching television!"

"Alright, alright, alright! Alexander, you coming or not? My feet are getting tired!" gasped Jacob the Centipede.

"OK, OK. I'm going! Let's go! It'll be a nice switch to get out of the motel for a couple of days, I guess," grunted Alexander the Bed Bug.

As the group of friends was walking away from The Wayside Motel, Krystal the Ant remarked, "'Dat really was a nice lil' joint. I don' know who be wantin' to pay 'da big bucks at dat' Grand Plaza when you could save a few Benjamins and stay at dat' Roach Motel."

With that, Alexander the Bed Bug, Wesley the Japanese Giant Hornet, Jacob the Centipede, Maddie the Stink Bug, Krystal the Ant, Annabelle the Giant Water Bug, Francesca the Rat, Genevieve the Louse, Julian the Maggot, Edward the Slug and Bethany the Cockroach hit the road towards The Trashy Hootenanny.

Chapter Twelve:

Bella the Termite

"I just don't know why your Aunt Ellen was so mean to you, Bethany," deliberated Genevieve the Louse. "That was terrible. I would have been crying my eyes out, but you're so much stronger than I am."

"Throughout the years, I've gotten used to it," replied Bethany the Cockroach. "Aunt Ellen has never liked anyone who is different from her, disagrees with her, or chases after their dreams. She has been stuck at The Roach Motel her entire life — never traveling or grasping opportunity. And that's fine, if that's your choice. But nobody should expect others to follow their same path."

The cockroach and the louse turned to each other and embraced. If one thing was certain, friendships were being forged on this journey. The group had just a few more friends to pick up before finally celebrating at The Trashy Hootenanny.

One of those friends was Bella the Termite, who lived in the school library at Pinkster Academy. Termites sometimes feed on books, when they're not munching on wood. Bella had found that the students of Pinkster Academy weren't really voracious readers — so she had her pick of the whole library!

"Hey, guys! I'm over here," called Bella the Termite, as she saw the group of bugs, accompanied by one dirty rat, enter the school library. The group had timed their visit perfectly, arriving in the middle of the night when the students, teachers and principal were all at home sleeping. "I'm eating this really cool book called *Gilbert the Grasshopper* — you'd all love it because it's about a bug! This wee, teeny, tiny grasshopper is so curious

that he jumps onto an airplane! Can you believe it??? Anyway, I won't ruin the ending for you... but I highly recommend it!"

"I don't understand," stated Wesley the Japanese Giant Hornet. "You read the books as you eat them?"

"Of course! I just love books so much…
and it breaks my heart that these children
aren't interested in reading them. So I read as
I eat! Read a page, eat a page. Read a page,
eat a page. This way, the books really aren't
going to waste."

"I jus' don' believe the children not be
reading 'dese books! When I was little, we be
goin' to da' schoo' li'berry all da' time. My
favorite was when dis' arthur came in. She be
so funny, readin' to us 'bout some purple
monkey. Whoda' ever thought 'bout 'dat?"

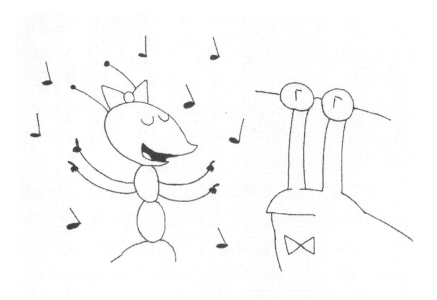

"I'm sorry, Krystal. Who came to visit?" asked Edward the Slug.

"Eddie, I don' know how I can say it any clearer. The arthur— ya' know? The arthur? The arthur writes the words, the arthur writes the words," sang Krystal in reply to Edward.

"She means the author! The writer of the book," interjected Jacob the Centipede, crossing his legs.

"Oh! I didn't understand…," trailed off Edward, looking like he might get angry. "But, anyway, that's very nice of an author to come visit your school, Krystal. It must have been very special for you."

"It is! It is! I read a book every day after 'dat. Got me so excited 'bout lit'ratcher."

"I'm really hungry!" bawled Maddie the Stink Bug, interrupting the conversation about the benefits of reading. She turned toward Bella the Termite and continued, "I wasn't hungry until you were flipping through that book, Gilbert the Grasshopper. I thought I saw a pretzel on one of the pages. I just love pretzels. They're so good with butter or cheddar cheese or sugar or cinnamon or salt or mustard or chocolate or sprinkles or moldy mayonnaise… oh, I'm making my hunger worse! Do you think I could try a little bite of book? Just a little. I promise!"

"Good, Lord. Please help 'dis chile'!" lamented Krystal the Ant, shaking her head at Maddie's appetite.

"I don't see any problem with that. But you need to read the page before you eat the page! That's my only rule," said Bella. Bella saw Maddie turn her head down in shame. "Here. This page of Gilbert the Grasshopper is very easy. Only six words — and the words repeat. I'm sure you will do very well."

Maddie squinted her eyes, getting her wide body right in between the pages of the book. "This says… j… juuu… jum… p… jump! It says jump!"

"Very good, go on…" assured Bella.

"Jump, jump, jump! Then, it reads… hooo… no, that's not right. It says hop! Hop, hop, hop! So the whole page is jump, jump, jump and hop, hop, hop! That was easy! I can read!" exclaimed Maddie, excited at her accomplishment. All the bugs clapped, encouraging their friend.

"Now, you get your reward," said Bella, tearing the page out of the book, handing it to Maddie.

Opening her mouth as wide as it would go, Maddie took a big bite of paper. And then another. And another. She was chewing and chewing and chewing. Finally, she swallowed. And then she took another bite! This Stink Bug was going to eat the whole page!

"Wow! I didn't know paper tasted so good! And I'd bet it's really good for you, too. Maybe I'll go on the paper diet," planned Maddie.

"Gurrrrrl, you think jus' 'bout anything tastes good," remarked Krystal.

With that, Bella the Termite, Alexander the Bed Bug, Wesley the Japanese Giant

Hornet, Jacob the Centipede, Maddie the
Stink Bug, Krystal the Ant, Annabelle the
Giant Water Bug, Francesca the Rat,
Genevieve the Louse, Julian the Maggot,
Edward the Slug and Bethany the Cockroach
hit the road towards The Trashy Hootenanny.

Chapter Thirteen:

Rosemarie the Spider

The dozen friends continued their journey through the night. Edward wanted to arrive at The Garden of Good and Plenty at sunrise. At this one stop, they would pick up three more hootenanny guests. Gardens are a popular place for many bugs and insects — and this one was no different. Flowers, fruits and vegetables were all in abundance at this garden, which supplied a local market. Of course, the group intended to steer clear of those nasty-smelling flowers.

"Here's the thing about Rosemarie: she never stays in one place, always weaving a new web," said Genevieve the Louse.

"Weave? Somebody say weave?" piped in Krystal the Ant.

"Anyway, her webs are always beautiful. And with the morning dew, sunlight beating down, it should be fairly easy to spot!" squeaked Genevieve.

"Did you know about Rosemarie's pet?" asked Jacob the Centipede.

"A spider has a pet? Now that's a new one," sneered Wesley the Japanese Giant Hornet.

"She keeps a pet fly! Apparently, she caught this fly named Bernard in her web one day. Before she could kill it, he started talking

to her. Rosemarie is rarely able to keep
friends. Let's face it," said Jacob. "Spiders
aren't the prettiest things around. So Bernard
started talking to her and she made a deal
with him. If she let him live, he would be her
friend forever and visit her every single day!"

"And so he does? He visits her? What if
he gets stuck in her web?" pondered Julian
the Maggot.

"She untangles him and lets him go. It's
a very awkward relationship, but they seem to
get along fine," said Jacob. "I just can't help

but wonder what might happen one day if Rosemarie is very, very hungry. Bye, bye, Bernie?"

"Hey! There's a spider web ahead! See it hanging in between the two stalks of corn?" exclaimed Francesca the Rat. "Could that be Rosemarie?"

As the group cautiously approached, they saw a fly buzzing around the web. He would spin and swirl and whip around the web, yet always avoid it. In the middle of the web sat a plump spider, holding a tiny, steaming mug. When she saw the group approaching, Rosemarie nearly spilled her drink in excitement.

"Wow! There's a whole bunch of you! We're all going to the hootenanny? This is going to be the night of my life!" prattled Rosemarie as she descended from her web. "Sorry, let me just finish this java. Bernard is such a sweetheart. He goes to the farmer's house every morning and steals me a few drips of coffee. I don't know what I'd do without that fly!"

Jacob and Wesley looked at each other, mouthing the word, "weird."

"Rosemarie, can you tell us a little more about The Garden of Good and Plenty?" asked Genevieve the Louse.

"Why, sure! The garden is huge — about as big as a football field. We have everything you could possibly imagine. Strawberries, potatoes, corn, green beans, tomatoes. The decorations are lovely, too. Scarecrows, giant ceramic mushrooms, and fairies! The farmers look so peaceful while they pick weeds, prune flowers and gather their grown produce, the warm sun brightening their day. Honestly, this garden is the best place on Earth and I couldn't imagine living anywhere else."

"Blah, blah, blah… I thought spiders s'posed to weave words into they webs n'stuff," said Krystal. "Rosie's web be lookin' all boring."

"That only happens in fiction!" screamed Rosemarie, throwing her tiny coffee mug on the ground. "And don't you call me Rosie."

"Apologies on behalf of Krystal. She has a habit of shortening words and names," interjected Edward.

"She just think she fancy because of 'dose eight legs. Well, Jacob gots you beat, sweet cheeks," nagged Krystal, trying to further her argument.

"I will crush you, Antsy Pantsy! I WILL CRUSH YOU!!!" bellowed Rosemarie, tears flowing from her eyes. Suddenly, Bernard the Fly swooped in, placing his wings around the spider's front left leg.

"There, there… it'll be ok, sweetheart," promised Bernard.

"I just want to have friends and be popular!" sobbed Rosemarie, the tears starting to dry up.

"I promise you that Krystal didn't mean any of it. She just likes to test people when she first meets them… she did it to all of us. Actually, she is really cool once you get to know her!" offered Annabelle the Giant Water Bug. "I think we should be on our way!"

With that, Rosemarie the Spider, Bella the Termite, Alexander the Bed Bug, Wesley the Japanese Giant Hornet, Jacob the Centipede, Maddie the Stink Bug, Krystal the Ant, Annabelle the Giant Water Bug, Francesca the Rat, Genevieve the Louse, Julian the Maggot, Edward the Slug and Bethany the Cockroach hit the road towards The Trashy Hootenanny.

Chapter Fourteen:

Landon the Millipede

"So I don' get it, Jake. You is a centipede and Landon be a millipede. What da' difference?" asked Krystal.

"It's kinda confusing, Krystal. You see, Landon and I are both arthropods. That means we have a lot of body segments. But I only have one pair of legs per body segment— and Landon has two! But even though he has two sets of legs per segment, I move really, really fast. And Landon moves slowly and burrows," explained Jacob.

"Where do you think we should look for him?" asked Maddie. "I think maybe we should go by the potatoes! I just love, love, love, love, love potatoes! They are so good cut up and fried. Or mashed with moldy sour cream! The tastiest is when you bake them with butter and then put rotten cheese on top! Or potato pancakes! Or potato soup!"

"I think you best be goin' to look by 'da green beans," remarked Krystal.

"As much as we don't want to do this, I think we might need to look for Landon by the rosebushes," said Rosemarie the Spider. "At this time of year, the farmers pile lots of mulch around the bases of the bushes, to give them protection through the winter. And, as Jacob so kindly pointed out, millipedes like to burrow — and they also like cool, damp places. That mulch will be retaining a lot of water from our storm last week."

"Wow, Rosemarie. I am quite impressed with your vast knowledge of rose bushes and gardening tactics," observed Edward the Slug. "How did you become so well-versed?"

"My mother was in love with roses. That's why she named me Rosemarie. Marie was my grandmother's name. And my mother's passion in life was smelling the roses," recalled Rosemarie.

"Ooooooohhhhhh… noooooooooo… I think I'm gonna be sick if we keep talking about the smell of flowers… it's basically the

grossest thing ever," moaned Genevieve the
Louse, holding her stomach.

"Now, now, now — to each their own,"
said Rosemarie.

"To each 'dey own? Whatchu' talkin'
'bout, Rosemarie?" asked Krystal.

"To each their own. It means that there's
always going to be differences in opinion. I
might like something that you don't. And you

might like something that I don't. And that's fine — it's what makes each of us our own, unique, individual self!" explained Rosemarie.

"I kinda like 'dat spida' after all," said Krystal, turning to Jacob. "'Dat right 'dere is a sensible way of living."

And so the conversation went as the group of friends made their way through the vast Garden of Good and Plenty. First, they climbed around giant pumpkins, which were just about to be picked for Halloween! Then, they swung around tall vines of grapes, about to be sold to a local winemaker. After that, they strolled through the cornfield, as Rosemarie explained that this was corn specifically engineered to be popcorn! Finally, they came to a field of strawberries… as far as the eye could see.

"OMG! These strawberries remind me of an episode of one of my favorite television shows! It's called The Amazing Adventures of Joe and Nick," said Julian, as the gang traveled through the strawberries. "They met this woman, her name was AnnMarie. Isn't

that weird? We have Rosemarie and
AnnMarie. Anyway, Nick and Joe were on a
cruise ship in Egypt and they met AnnMarie
at dinner. One night, for dessert, they were
served chocolate-covered strawberries. Now,
AnnMarie was from Germany, but she lived
in Canada. So she had a very thick German
accent."

"Do 'dis story have an end?" asked an
exasperated Krystal.

"Let him finish! It's making time go by,"
said Jacob.

"AnnMarie said, 'von time, ve vere
valking tru zee vorest. Okay? And zen, ve zee
a vlack vear. Okay? Ve vollowed zee vlack
vear tru zee voods. Okay? Until ve reach a
strawverry patch,'" said Julian, in his best
German accent. "'In zee strawverry patch…
okay? Zee vlack vear ate zo many
strawverries. Okay? And zen? Zee vlack vear
fell azleep in zee strawverries! Okay?!?!?'"

"Aw, no! 'Dis boy be trippin," spluttered
Krystal.

"Hahahahahah! That was the best impersonation EVER, Julian," complimented Annabelle.

"I didn't know you were so talented," flirted Genevieve, batting her eyelashes.

"It was pointless! The whole thing was pointless!" huffed Wesley, throwing his wings in the air.

"Not really, Wesley. Look ahead— we are already at the rosebushes! So Julian's lovely story made the time pass by. It's a good lesson to learn. When you're traveling, sometimes you just need mindless entertainment," informed Edward. "Not... not to say that you are actually mindless, Julian. Genevieve! What on Earth are you doing!?!"

"Well, I just decided to stuff a couple of strawberry seeds in my nose to block the rose smell," squeaked Genevieve, her voice altered by her muffled nose.

"Is it working?" asked Francesca.

"So far, so good. I can't smell a thing!" replied Genevieve.

"Here is the plan," declared Edward. "Let's split up — Rosemarie, you can lead one group and I'll lead the other. Each group can walk around the perimeter of the rosebush patch and meet on the other side. Let's see… I'll take Wesley, Bella, Annabelle, Julian, Bethany and… Krystal."

"I know 'dat's right! Woot! Woot! I'm on Eddie's team!" celebrated Krystal, jumping up and down.

"Both of the teams are equal, Krystal. Nobody is better than anyone else," said Edward. "Rosemarie, you'll take Alexander, Jacob, Maddie, Francesca and Genevieve. We will go to the left — your group can go to the right."

The two groups of friends went their separate ways, in their search for Landon the Millipede. They looked under pieces of mulch. They were careful not to get poked by the thorns on the bushes. Julian and Annabelle complained about the smell, while Genevieve smiled the entire way, two strawberry seeds plugging her nostrils. Annabelle and Wesley fluttered above, getting an aerial view. Krystal and Julian rustled through a pile of browning rose leaves. All of this hard work was to no avail… Landon couldn't be found. Soon, the two teams met up, on the far side of the field of rose bushes.

"I'm stumped! I thought he would at least hear us and come out to the edge," said Rosemarie. "But I've got an idea. Hold on!"

Swiftly, the spider began climbing the nearest rosebush. The others watched as she swung around and up the branches, delicately avoiding thorns. Rosemarie quickly ascended, reaching higher and higher in the bush, until the group could no longer see her.

"Where did she go?" asked Jacob.

"I have no idea," answered Edward.

"Beats me," said Francesca.

"Not a clue," piped in Alexander.

"Maybe she went to pick up breakfast!" exclaimed Maddie.

"Look! She's coming back! She's coming back!" clapped Bethany.

Sure enough, a silvery thread was carrying Rosemarie with the wind, down toward the ground. It was magical, the way she appeared to float in the air, carried by the silk. But there was something flying next to Rosemarie… tiny wings fluttering very quickly, two antennas, a stinger, stripes of yellow… sure enough, Rosemarie was accompanied by a bee!

"This is my friend, Humphrey," explained Rosemarie, landing on the soft ground. "He has some information about Landon that he is willing to share!"

"Landon is in the very center of the rosebushes!" panted Humphrey, who was out of breath from his flight. "What you need to do is get to the yellow bush, turn right. When you cross over the pile of rotting egg shells, take a left. Then, when you come to the pink roses, turn left again. You'll then go around the giant stack of banana peels and turn right. Now, this is where it gets tricky— there is a roundabout. Two big cones are in place, protecting the prized Empress Josephine of

France Roses. You'll have to circumnavigate around those, passing to the right of the first one and then around the left of the second one. Finally, you'll see the brightest red roses you've ever imagined! That is where you'll find Landon."

"I sho' hope somebody can 'member all 'dat," huffed Krystal.

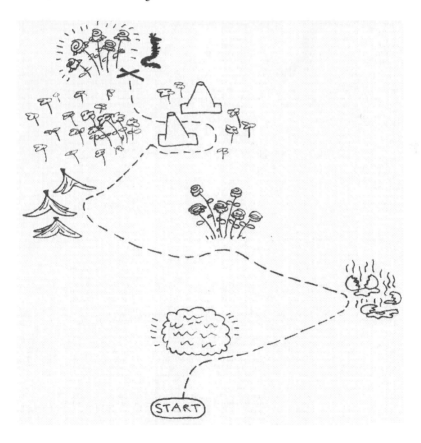

"Actually… I remember ALL of it," bragged Francesca. "Yellow bushes, right. Egg shells, left. Pink, left. Bananas, right. Roundabout, right and left. The end."

"Now that we know, let's go! Time, time, time!" exclaimed Edward. "Oh, and thank you so very much for all of the wonderful information. It is such highly appreciated, valuable instruction. Francesca, lead the way." Everyone in the group shared glances at each other, surprised that Edward was relinquishing his role as leader, even for a moment.

The thirteen friends, following Francesca's long, dirty tail, made their way, single file through the forest of rosebushes. Sure enough, they saw the beautiful yellow roses first. Shortly thereafter, a pungent smell of rotting egg filled the air, overtaking even the scent of the roses. A crunching sound began to accompany the peaceful quiet of the roses.

"Maddie, you really be eatin' some egg shells?" asked Krystal.

"Well, since we couldn't go by the potatoes and have some potato chips, this might satisfy my taste for something crunchy!" responded Maddie.

"Oh, those pink roses are so gorgeous!" swooned Genevieve. Just as the words were out of her mouth, Wesley the Japanese Giant Hornet fluttered his wings, taking off toward the roses above.

"Here, my pretty louse… a pink rose to show you my affection," said Wesley, handing her a single rose petal. Genevieve blushed. Julian seethed. The group approached the largest pile of banana peels that any of them had ever seen.

"I'm watchin' you, Maddie— keep yo' jaws away from da' bananas. Those are for da' roses!" said Krystal, casting a disapproving look toward the stink bug.

Finally, the group passed around the giant cones, which protected very expensive roses for the winter months. And there, directly in front of them, was just what Humphrey described— the brightest red roses. As Francesca approached the base of the bush, she screamed at the top of her lungs!

"What's wrong?" asked a worried Edward.

"I didn't think Landon was gonna be so ugly!" confessed Francesca.

"Hey! I didn't call you ugly — and you're not exactly the prettiest thing I've ever seen," said Landon the Millipede, crawling his way out from his burrowed nest underneath the red roses. He walked to the line of his friends and began high-fiving all of them with his tiny legs. "How exciting is this?!?! A hootenanny with the whole gang!! It's gonna be so much fun!"

"Maddie, no!" shrieked Rosemarie the Spider. Maddie was sitting atop a giant wooden barrel, which was labeled *tea*.

"What? I love tea — and I'm parched. I hope it's sweet tea," said Maddie, jumping into the barrel before anyone could stop her.

"That tea is anything but sweet!" exclaimed Rosemarie. "The farmers mix chicken manure with water. They use this to fertilize some of the crops… and they call it *tea*!'"

"I think this tea has gone bad," said Maddie the Stink Bug, emerging from the barrel, dripping in brown water.

With that, Landon the Millipede, Rosemarie the Spider, Bella the Termite, Alexander the Bed Bug, Wesley the Japanese Giant Hornet, Jacob the Centipede, Maddie the Stink Bug, Krystal the Ant, Annabelle the Giant Water Bug, Francesca the Rat, Genevieve the Louse, Julian the Maggot, Edward the Slug and Bethany the Cockroach hit the road towards The Trashy Hootenanny.

Chapter Fifteen:

Simon the Earthworm

"If dey' is one thing I can say about 'dis group, it's we gots lots a legs," said Krystal, looking back and forth at the length of Landon's body, accompanied by all those legs!

"Landon, any word on where we can find Simon the Earthworm?" asked Edward.

"Yes! I just saw him three days ago and he was worried you wouldn't be able to find him. So he told me that he'd be in the potato field, right by the northwestern edge," said Landon. "He said to look for the stack of newspapers. Which didn't make much sense to me. But he's a pretty smart dude. So I'm sure it will work out. Shall we? We will be at the potatoes in a flash!"

Krystal looked at Maddie, saying, "Don' you even say it."

"I'm not hungry, anyway. Those egg shells are nothing but protein. So I'm stuffed!" huffed Maddie, crossing her arms in defiance.

With Landon leading the way, the group traveled out of the forest of rosebushes. The Trashy Hootenanny, now just hours away, was getting the friends more excited than ever. There was definitely a pep in the step of all the tiny feet climbing over the dirt. Walking along the edge of the potato field, Wesley spotted the stack of newspapers first.

"Hello. My name is Simon! I'm an oithwoim. I'm from New Joisey!" said the

earthworm, slithering along beside the
newspaper.

"What he be sayin'? I swear I can't take
it when people don' use 'dey words!" shouted
Krystal.

"Oh… hahahah… I forgot. I'll drop the
accent," said Simon. "Sometimes I forget that
I don't live in New Jersey anymore. Since I
got shipped out in that fish bait container, I'll
never see that place again."

"Fish bait?" asked Genevieve.

"Yeah, I got scooped up and put into
this tiny little container with dozens of other
worms. We were gonna swim with the fishes!
I escaped and ended up here, in The Garden
of Good and Plenty. Best move I've ever
made," explained Simon.

"Thank God you escaped! That would
be terrible, being eaten by a fish!" shrieked
Maddie. "I mean, do earthworms even taste
good?"

"Never mind all that, Simon. What do
you know about this hootenanny?" asked
Edward the Slug.

"Here is what I know— it's all my idea, that's for sure! I read a very interesting article in the newspaper that will benefit all of us very, very much," said Simon.

"In the newspaper? Why are you reading newspapers?" wondered Julian.

"It passes the time, young Julian. The farmers use newspaper around the potato plants. It keeps in the moisture and also prevents weeds from growing. So, I make sure I read as much as I can every single day," said Simon.

"That explains the pile of newspapers!" chirped Annabelle, stating the obvious.

"A few weeks back, there was an article about this little boy. The boy's name was

Massimiliano. He was in the news because he wouldn't clean his room," said Simon. "Now, I know what you're thinking — lots of kids have dirty rooms. But, in this article, the mother mentioned that it was the worst thing she had ever seen! And the worst for her... means the best for us.

"Since the boy wouldn't clean his room, the mother didn't know what to do. So, she turned towards this new method of punishment, where the kiddos have to stand on a street corner with a sign! The picture in

the newspaper was classic! There stood little Massimiliano, holding a sign with big, painted letters, reading 'I Won't Clean My Room.' The look on the poor kid's face… I felt kinda bad for him. But then I thought of the possibilities! It's been such a long time since any bugs in this area have had a hootenanny. And this kid's room would be the perfect location."

"Wow! I think this is awesome, Simon. You're like a detective!" said Maddie.

"I agree. It reminds me of one of my favorite television shows, Insect Hoarder 3: Overflowing Garbage," said Julian. "They have all these abandoned rooms full of junk… and it would be so much fun to roam around in there, seeing what kind of disgusting things I could find. This might be the next best thing!"

"However, what if this Massimiliano child has already cleaned his room? That public shaming punishment probably worked. We will get there and the room will be clean and then all of this is for nothing!" countered Edward the Slug.

"I know newspapers can be a little out of date. But iPhones aren't! Yesterday, the farmer was distracted, placing fresh newspapers around the potatoes. So I strolled over to his iPhone and did some digging in public records. Sure enough, the house is on a list to be inspected. The city may condemn the property — all because this kid didn't clean his room!"

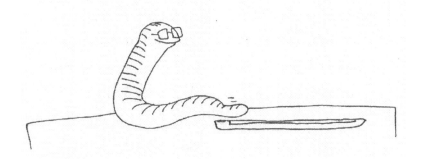

"Very good work, Simon! How did you know how to use an iPhone?" asked Genevieve.

"Well, Steve Jobs was right, ya' know? Man was a genius. It's all very intuitive. It should come right to you," replied Simon.

"Good work, indeed! But I do have one last question: how do we get in the house without the humans noticing?" asked Bethany.

"This is where I did a little more digging, so-to-speak. I turned to my friend Kyoung Park Lee. He is an Asian King Snake... from North Korea. Kyoung was accidentally shipped here in a container full of pears. But that's beside the point. He is very smart with computers— and especially good when it comes to hacking other computers. So he snuck into the farmer's house one evening and went to work, hacking the computer of Massimiliano's mother," explained Simon.

"How does he do that?!?" gasped Maddie.

"According to Kyoung Park Lee, most people use the password *MeLoveYouLongTime*. So that's what he tries first. Other than that, he keeps his secrets. Anyway, in her calendar, the family is scheduled to attend a wedding this afternoon, with the reception lasting until midnight at least. So as long as we arrive by 2:00 PM, we can watch from afar, wait for them to leave… and then begin The Trashy Hootenanny!!!"   "Brilliant! The whole thing is simply brilliant!" exclaimed Edward the Slug. "Shall we proceed, then?"

"Sounds good to me," answered Simon.

"Aren't we missing one person?"

"One more pick-up and then we are complete!" answered Edward.

With that, Simon the Earthworm, Landon the Millipede, Rosemarie the Spider,

Bella the Termite, Alexander the Bed Bug, Wesley the Japanese Giant Hornet, Jacob the Centipede, Maddie the Stink Bug, Krystal the Ant, Annabelle the Giant Water Bug, Francesca the Rat, Genevieve the Louse, Julian the Maggot, Edward the Slug and Bethany the Cockroach hit the road towards The Trashy Hootenanny.

Chapter Sixteen:

Leah the Flea

"What on Earth is that racket?" complained Wesley the Japanese Giant Hornet, hearing dogs bark as they approached a small, brick building. On the building hung a sign, reading, "DOG WARDEN."

"All of these dogs are homeless?" asked Genevieve the Louse.

"Yes, they are mostly strays, Genevieve. Some have been turned in by people who can't take care of them properly. But all of them are looking for a good home," explained Bethany the Cockroach.

Suddenly, a side door opened and there was a blur of activity as 15 dogs ran out into the fenced outdoor enclosure. They all looked very happy, playing with each other, tails wagging, treats and toys flying into the air. There were big dogs and small dogs, fluffy dogs and dogs with short hair, white dogs, black dogs, and tan dogs. One of them, a medium-sized dog, that looked like a mix of several breeds, approached the fence where

the gang of friends had gathered. He was sniffing the fence line, poking his nose just inches away from Francesca the Rat.

Squinting at the tip of the dog's nose, Alexander the Bed Bug spotted her first. "There— it's a flea! It's Leah!" shrieked Alexander.

"Hey y'all!" yelled Leah, from the dog's nose.

"How did you spot her, Alexander?" asked Landon the Millipede.

"I've got really good eyesight. In fact, my momma always said, 'You could spot a freckle on a flea's butt.' I guess she was right!" laughed Alexander.

"You listen here, Zipper. You're such a good boy," said Leah to the dog, standing on his nose and looking him in the eyes. "I hope this is goodbye. I'll be back soon— but I really hope that you're not here. I wish that you are cozied up in a nice warm house, with a couple of kids and maybe even another dog. You can run in the leaves during the day, snuggle up with your family in front of a fireplace in the evening— and choose which comfy human bed you want to take over at night. There will be lots of food. And the kids will sneak you table scraps, I'm sure. Every good dog gets a good home… and you deserve the best home. I love you, Zipper."

Leah the Flea leaned forward and kissed the dog square on the nose. He bent low towards the ground, allowing Leah to jump off and join her friends. Zipper let out a soft whimper as he watched his friend go away.

Leah turned back and said, "Don't you do that, sweet boy! You are going to find a lot better friends than me in your life. I promise! You'll always remember me by that bright, red collar I got for you.

"Howdy! I know most of y'all," said Leah, turning to the gathered group of bugs.

"But for those of you that I don't know, my name is Leah the Flea from Tennessee!"

"Hi Leah!" said Genevieve.

"Nice to meet you, Leah," added Alexander.

"I don' be knowin' nothin' 'bout no fleas, but she seem nice enough," nagged Krystal.

"Oh, bless your heart! So, we fixin' to leave for this hootenanny soon? I want to get out of here so Zipper can go make some new friends!" called Leah.

"We do need to be moving as soon as possible. The house isn't that far— but it's nearly noon," said Simon.

"Finally! Someone else on this trip that understands the importance of punctuality!" asserted Edward.

The group of friends began the final leg of their journey. Leah the Flea turned back just one time, before leaving the parking lot of the dog warden. A grin passed across her face, as she saw Zipper playing with the other dogs. Although she hated to leave him, she knew he'd be just fine.

"Do you like living at the dog warden, Leah? Seems like it would be fun— a lot of action!" said Wesley, sidling up beside the flea as they traveled down the neatly-kept sidewalk.

"Oh, sure I do. But it is difficult sometimes when friends come and go. I meet so many new dogs and cats. But I know that I only get to have them in my life for a little while. And that's okay, because when they first arrive at the shelter, they need a friend more than anything in the world!" explained Leah. "Not to change the subject... but what do you think of that slug, Edward? I reckon, with that attitude, he ain't worth two dead flies."

"Not worth two dead flies? I don't understand," said Wesley.

"Oh, I'm sorry. Bless your heart. It's a southern thing. I just don't trust that parasite. Tellin' everybody what to do and when to do it… once we get down yonder, in the holler, to the hootenanny, I'm steering clear of him. Dumber than a box of rocks, I tell 'ya."

"Yeah, not many of us like Edward all that much… but he's been our leader throughout and hasn't steered us in the wrong direction. That's why we tolerate his behavior," piped in Genevieve.

"Well, that millipede is so ugly, we'd have to tie a pork chop around his neck to get the dogs to play with him. And Julian… he is cute enough, but he wasn't blessed with a brain, God love 'em. But that ant… Krystal was her name? I declare, that girl is just sweeter'n Tupelo honey," smiled Leah.

"Krystal? Sweet? I love sweets!" exclaimed Maddie, drawing laughter from the rest of the group. "I love chocolate and cake and whipped cream and icing and candy and pie and biscuits and pudding and Jell-O and bubblegum and cookies and pastries and cupcakes and…"

With that, Leah the Flea, Simon the Earthworm, Landon the Millipede, Rosemarie the Spider, Bella the Termite, Alexander the Bed Bug, Wesley the Japanese Giant Hornet, Jacob the Centipede, Maddie the Stink Bug, Krystal the Ant, Annabelle the Giant Water Bug, Francesca the Rat, Genevieve the Louse,

Julian the Maggot, Edward the Slug and Bethany the Cockroach hit the road towards The Trashy Hootenanny.

Chapter Seventeen:

The Trashy Hootenanny

"This is the house," said Simon the Earthworm, as the cast of characters crouched behind a large, decorative rock in the front yard. Sure enough, on the front lawn stood a posting about the upcoming inspection. "We are going to sit tight here and wait for them to leave. The wedding ceremony starts at 2:00 PM. It's 1:18 now. So they should be leaving soon."

"What are you hoping to find at the hootenanny?" asked Jacob, turning to Rosemarie.

"I'm sure there will be some nice, fresh, juicy, plump flies flying around," responded Rosemarie, who turned to Krystal. "Krystal, what are you the most excited about?"

"I is really hoping we can find some sushi. Everybody be talkin' 'bout how good it is. I gotsta try it!" exclaimed Krystal.

"Shhhh! Shhhh! The front door just opened!" said Edward. Silently, each of the bugs poked their head over the giant rock.

First, a slim, well-dressed, blonde-haired teenage girl stepped onto the front porch. She was soon accompanied by a tall and slender middle-aged woman. The woman appeared to be agitated, pacing back-and-forth, looking at her watch. The girl took a seat on the front porch steps, tapping her toes in anxiousness. Finally, the woman had enough.

"Massssimillllliano D'Milllllllliiiiioooooo! Get out here right this minute! We are going to be late for your cousin's wedding," screamed the mother.

"Yeah, I'm tired of waiting! These shoes are already killing my feet," mumbled the girl.

"Maybe you'd rather stay here and clean that pigsty of a room you live in," shouted the mother.

Minutes passed by before a shadow appeared in the doorway. Finally, a boy emerged. He was just an average-looking boy, perhaps 12 years old. He wore a suit, complete with a tie and jacket. His sand-colored hair was messed up with gel, just like all the kids were doing. But he was wearing tennis shoes! Tennis shoes with a suit?

"I told you about the shoes, Massimiliano. This isn't a school dance where you get to flash a little personality. This is your cousin's wedding day! You cannot wear tennis shoes!" implored the mother.

"Mom, I can't find my dress shoes anywhere," protested Massimiliano.

"And you know exactly why you can't find them, don't you? It's that disgusting room!" retorted the mother.

"I'll clean it tomorrow," replied Massimiliano.

"Yeah— and you've been saying that for three years now. Go get in the car," said the mother, her teeth gritting together in anger.

"THREE years? Three years?!?!? This is gonna be awesome!" shrieked Julian the Maggot.

"Shush! We can't be seen — or heard!" roared Edward.

The sixteen friends watched as the family trio got into their sparkling SUV. Slowly, the vehicle backed down the driveway and onto the street. All eyes were on the car until it reached the end of the street and turned right, out of view. The friends turned to look at each other. Could it be? Was it finally time? Excitement overcame each of them as they realized Simon's plan had worked flawlessly.

"Let's GO!" yelled Francesca, charging the house, her brown tail bouncing behind her. The rat jumped onto an eavestrough, climbing up the side of the house. "I'm heading in through the chimney!"

"Ohmygosh! Somebody pinch me! I know for a fact that I can smell molded mushroom pizza!" growled Maddie, the hunger in her stomach exponentially growing. The stink bug was headed for the front window, expertly squeezing herself through a hole in the screen.

So it went.

Bethany the Cockroach, Landon the Millipede and Jacob the Centipede all snuck in through a crack in the foundation. Edward the Slug and Julian the Maggot both went in underneath the garage door. Wesley the Japanese Giant Hornet and Annabelle the Giant Water Bug used their wings to their advantage, flying up to where the cable television line entered the home, burrowing their way inside through the hole. Simon the Earthworm, Bella the Termite and Alexander the Bed Bug all proceeded to the back of the house, climbing their way inside through the dryer vent. Leah and Krystal entered the house through the crawl space, accessible by a tiny window close to the ground. Genevieve hitched a ride on Rosemarie's back, as she climbed quickly up the side of the house, slipping in through the attic.

All of the friends followed the scent coming from Massimiliano's room, meeting up in front of his door. Simon the Earthworm took a spot in front of all his guests. "Ladies and Gentlemen, insects and bugs, rats of all ages… I welcome you to The Trashy Hootenanny!"

To punctuate his welcoming speech, Simon turned around and pushed open the door to the room. Eyes widened as the door to the room slowly creaked open. Piles of garbage and dirty laundry were strewn about, crumpled-up homework littered the desk, plates and dishes were everywhere. And the smell? Well, the smell was delectable. Each member of the group scurried into the room, shooting off into different directions.

"This hootenanny needs some music," shouted Wesley, hovering near the radio. The hornet dive-bombed the power button. Loud sound filled the room.

"It's going down, I'm yelling timber! You better move, you better dance! Let's make a night, you won't remember," came the shrill voice from the speaker.

"Ooooohhhhh I love this song!" screeched Maddie. "The girl that sings it would fit in really well here at The Trashy Hootenanny. She seems so nice!"

"Jackpot!" warbled Julian the Maggot, his voice coming from inside a dirty backpack in the far corner of the room. "I found a hardboiled egg! It's been here since the 2nd day of school, according to the papers I found with it. Which makes it... two months old?"

Julian opened the container and the scent instantly took over the room. "Holy moly, this is fantastic! I've never had an egg this rotten before... yummmmmmmmmmmmmmmy!" gloated Julian.

"I don't know what this is, but it's amazing," said Annabelle, sitting on the carpet, where a tube of candy lipstick had melted into the fiber. The Giant Water Bug was definitely enjoying her sweet treat, licking and nibbling on the sugary substance.

"I coulda' swore these looked like mouse turds," said Leah the Flea, eating a small black pebble. "Whatever they are, they're dry'r'n a popcorn fart!"

"Oh! That was in the newspaper article! The mother said she sprinkled black rice all over the room, so that the boy would think there was a rat or mouse in the room! So you're eating black rice," explained Simon.

"Rat? Well, they've got the real thing now and I'm loving life!" hooted Francesca. The rat was underneath the bed, gnawing away at what appeared to be a naked Barbie doll.

"Weird. Why would this kid have a naked Barbie doll?" pondered Landon the Millipede.

"Why would he have 44 almost-empty soda cans?" asked Jacob the Centipede, tipping over the cans one at a time to drink the remains of Pepsi, Coca-Cola, Mountain Dew and more.

"There's a fungus among us!" squealed Bethany the Cockroach, poking her head out of a filthy tube sock. "There is some stank mold growing in these socks. The stankiest, stinkiest, grossest foot fungus I've ever tasted. I'm in heaven!"

All the friends stopped to stare when they heard a crunching sound coming from the wall above the bed. There sat Bella the Termite, scraping something off the wall with her teeth.

"Bella, whatchu got up 'dere?" asked Krystal, who was chomping on a hardening yogurt that she had found in the same backpack as the egg.

"Boogers! Lots and lots of dried boogers on the wall. I guess he ran out of tissue," said Bella, gobbling down the green goobers.

"I'm not usually such a pig, but I don't know any better way to do this," said Edward. The slug, standing on top of a pile of comic books, took a deep breath and then jumped off the ledge, landing in an old plate of spaghetti. "The Italians are pure genius!

Pasta and tomato sauce and meat and parmesan cheese… mix it all together, let it sit on a plate for six weeks… I'd like to see them beat that on Iron Insect Chef!"

"Hey! That's one of my favorite television shows," called Julian from the other side of the room, where he was devouring a piece of red-and-green-wrapped candy, hair sticking to it in places. Judging by the colors, the candy had been there since the previous Christmas.

"Wow! It's an iPhone! I've never seen one of these in person before," said Landon, looking at the shiny object resting on the bed. "Simon! You know how to use this— come take a selfie with me!"

"What on Earth is that?" shrieked Genevieve the Louse, watching Rosemarie eating something absolutely disgusting.

"It looks like an old hamster carcass… mmmmm… tastes like one, too!" oozed the spider, chomping away on the old flesh of the hamster.

"How would a hamster carcass just appear in a kid's bedroom?" wondered Annabelle.

"I'm sure the hamster got out of its cage and just got lost in the mess. Maybe it suffocated in the dirty laundry!" hollered Alexander the Bed Bug, who was scarfing down a bloody bandage he had found balled up in a pair of dirty underwear. "What does the hamster taste like?"

"I've tried it before," piped in Maddie. "Tastes like chicken."

"Humph. Hamsta'— da' udder white meat," joked Krystal.

Suddenly, the door to the bedroom swung open. The bugs, insects and Francesca were having such a grand time that they had forgotten to watch the clock — even Edward the Slug! Massimiliano's mother stood in the doorway, surveying the scene. When she laid eyes on the creatures in her son's bedroom, she let out the shrillest, most blood-curdling scream any of us had ever heard. Massimiliano and his sister ran to the bedroom door.

"Ohmygod, ohmygod, ohmygod…. Bugs! Lots and lots of bugs," screeched the sister, her feet hopping up and down in fear. Massimiliano's face turned white as he watched the scene before him. He leaned in closer to Maddie the Stink Bug, who was eating an olive she found in Massimiliano's wrestling shoes. The boy was holding his stomach, trying not to get sick at the sight of the disgusting little bug.

"I'll clean my room! I'll clean my room right this second!" shouted Massimiliano, bursting into tears.

"We gotsa' go!" declared Krystal.

Promptly, the friends all scurried. Francesca ran between the mother's legs. Maddie and Bella high-tailed it towards the crack in the closet floor. Jacob and Alexander did a quick whirl around the sister's feet, just to scare her a little. Wesley and Annabelle took to the air, zipping past Massimiliano's head. Landon and Julian, along with Edward, slithered under the bed, where they burrowed between the floor boards to make their great escape. Bethany and Simon sprinted up the wall to the window, where Leah and Krystal had already gathered. Rosemarie climbed straight up the wall towards the attic, Genevieve on her back.

Without warning, the spider stopped, turning to look at Massimiliano. "Thanks for the great time, kid… but maybe you'll learn to keep your room clean!" said Rosemarie.

With that, Leah the Flea, Simon the Earthworm, Landon the Millipede, Rosemarie the Spider, Bella the Termite, Alexander the Bed Bug, Wesley the Japanese Giant Hornet, Jacob the Centipede, Maddie the Stink Bug, Krystal the Ant, Annabelle the Giant Water Bug, Francesca the Rat, Genevieve the Louse, Julian the Maggot, Edward the Slug and Bethany the Cockroach hit the road towards home, having made a lifetime of memories with each other at The Trashy Hootenanny.

The End

A Note... from Nick and Joe

We hope you enjoyed reading The Trashy Hootenanny! For our first full-fledged chapter book, we were very excited to include some of our humor, along with teaching young readers about dialogue and dialect. We are hoping that this story will be the first in a series of "Hootenanny" books!

As always, we like to include some personal ties with our kid fans. There may be some familiar names within the story. And if you'd like to be included in a future release, post a pic of yourself, with your name, on our Facebook page at www.Facebook.com/PeteThePopcorn.

Finally, we held a contest for our fans. The challenge was to show your dirtiest kid rooms! The winner is featured on the back cover... but please enjoy these photos from others that entered.

Keep reading!
Nick and Joe

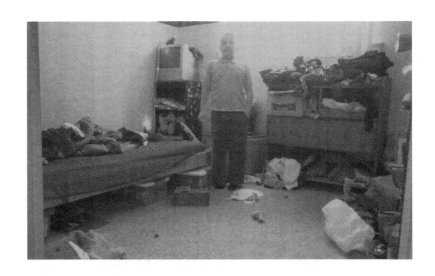

But wait! There's more! As a special surprise for our loyal readers... here is a preview chapter of our forthcoming release: *I'm Right Rita, a Sam Palowski Story.*

Chapter One...

By the way, my full name is Samantha. Maybe I shouldn't have left that part out in the beginning, but at least I'm telling you now. Do you want to learn a little bit about butternut squash? Well, sorry. But I have to tell you, anyway. This is a necessary part of the story, if you're going to read about Rita.

Every fall, trucks dot the fields in and around Beebeetown. Small trucks and big trucks, all filled to the brim with butternut squash. They come empty, they leave full. And then they come back. Empty and full, empty and full. Day after day, throughout the month of September. Growing up, I'd watch the trucks and think, where could all of this squash possibly be going? Who eats this much squash? How do they eat it? Where is the farthest place on the planet that

Beebeetown's squash has ended up? These are the questions of a young girl in Iowa.

Luckily, I've found out some of these answers, but others remain elusive. In my research, I found that Martha Stewart and Rachael Ray have had an impact on the amount of squash that is actually eaten. You see, most of it ends up painted silver or gold, or carved out and used for somebody's Halloween display. This is kind of weird, if you ask me. If this keeps up, pumpkins will go extinct!

You'd think that we'd eat a lot of squash here where it's grown. But we don't. The most my Mom has ever done with a squash is scoop out the seeds, fill it with hamburger and then bake it. She says it's healthier than meatloaf, because it's served inside of a vegetable. I have my doubts.

Call me crazy, but this squash mystery was really bugging me. So one beautiful May day after school, I marched down County Road S-5 (yes, that's how boring things are in Beebeetown — we can't even think up street names) to visit Mr. Bud Roberts. Bud owns 30% of all the squash farms in the area, so he knows his squash.

I traveled to his house just wanting to ask him where it goes… but I found out a lot more than I expected!

The Roberts Family lives in a large white house, surrounded by a green yard that is bigger than my school's football field. That square of green grass sits in the middle of fields, upon fields, of butternut squash. Leading to the house is a stone, dusty driveway with rose bushes planted on either side. Kathie, Bud's wife, is the President of the Beebeetown Rose Society. There are only two members of this exclusive club, her and Judy Vargas, so they swap President and Vice President jobs each year. Regardless, when I need to get a rose for my Mom's birthday, I know where to go.

I was passing exactly the 18th rosebush when I saw a vehicle parked in front of the wide stairway leading to the porch that wrapped around the home. The car wasn't familiar — in fact, it looked like it didn't belong at all! Large and black, with windows that I couldn't see through, this car was built to carry someone important, I was sure. Sometimes my Dad calls me "nosy," which I guess I am. After all, a reporter for SNN has to be! But I also try to be polite, so instead of opening the door to the car and checking out the contents, I tiptoed up the front porch steps and took a comfortable seat on the cushioned swing. Luckily for me and my nosiness, the swing was just outside of an open window. And I could hear everything perfectly!

"A factory? Right here in Beebeetown? You want to build a factory? I don't know how the town would react, Mr. Waters," said the voice of Bud Roberts. I knew it was Mr. Roberts, because he seems to sing everything he says. Really! Go back, and instead of reading that line, sing it out loud. That's what Bud Roberts sounds like when he speaks.

"It would really help the bottom line of my business, Bud. Plus, it would give this town a lot of jobs— jobs that it needs," said the voice that must have been Mr. Waters. He sounded like he was from some alien land, with an accent that was so rushed and harsh. "Instead of trucking all the squash to New York and then producing it, packaging it and shipping it back across the country, we could cut the cost and make it all right here!"

As the men spoke, I could almost feel my ears growing. However, I was sure that this conversation was not meant to be heard. While my ears were growing taller, I crouched lower and lower into the swing. If Mr. Roberts saw me, I would be in big trouble.

"But I just don't know if the town council will approve, Mr. Waters. There are very few projects that have ever gotten off the ground here in Beebeetown, I'm positive you can see that. The folks around here just don't want to change. They want to grow their squash, sell their squash... and then do it again the next year. Life stays simple that way."

"Bud, there are three votes on the town council. You are one of those votes, but you'd be selling me the land for the factory, so you'd have to recuse yourself from voting. Dan Jenkins and Sophia Sanders are friends of yours— they will support this! Your hands will be clean from the vote, you'll sell some land and I will guarantee purchase of 100% of your squash crop at every harvest. This is a win for everyone, Bud. And maybe you could even sell some more land when all these factory workers start moving in. They'll have to build their homes somewhere!"

"You're going to purchase 100% of my squash every year? That's millions of pounds of squash, Mr. Waters. This factory will make that much soup? I can't believe people really eat Butternut Squash Soup! And that much of it?!"

"Waters Brand Butternut Squash Soup is the wave of the future, Bud. People want healthy food. They want delicious food. And they want convenient food. Squash soup is the answer — and it will mean the rebirth of this town, too!"

"And you? You'll move here to Beebeetown and bring your family with you?"

"My lovely wife Suzanne and my daughter Rita will be coming to live here with me, full-time. I'm dedicating my soup to this town and I'm also dedicating my family to this town. Let's get this done, Bud. I will have my lawyers draw up a purchase plan for your property and an agreement for the sale of your annual squash harvest. Once we sign the paperwork, it will be approved by the town council and we'll be making Butternut Squash Soup in September! Deal?"

"Deal!"

With that, I heard the sound of two hands slapping, the beginning click of a firm handshake. Just as the screen door was opening, I swiftly kicked myself off the swing and over the porch railing. Scampering through the fields of growing squash, my mind was reeling. Butternut Squash Soup? A factory in Beebeetown? New houses for people moving in? I had the biggest story that Beebeetown has ever seen! My feet couldn't take me home quick enough — this breaking news wouldn't write itself!

Made in the USA
Middletown, DE
26 February 2017